Lots of things at the beach scared Sukie. Lots.

For Falon, Eleanor, Piper, and Geneva — C. C.

To Calvin, Strider, Scarlet, Solo, EJ, Mochi, Cooper, Liesel, Stella, Buster, Leo, and Guster, all good dogs some of the time! — L. M.

First edition 2017

Library of Congress Catalog Card Number pending
ISBN 978-0-7636-7542-4

17 18 19 20 21 22 CCP 10 9 8 7 6 5 4 3 2 1

Printed in Shenzhen, Guangdong, China

This book was typeset in Filosofia.
The illustrations were done in watercolor, acrylic, and pen and ink.

Candlewick Press
99 Dover Street
Somerville, Massachusetts 02144

visit us at www.candlewick.com

There Might Be Lobsters

illustrated by

CAROLYN CRIMI LAUREL MOLK

CANDLEWICK PRESS

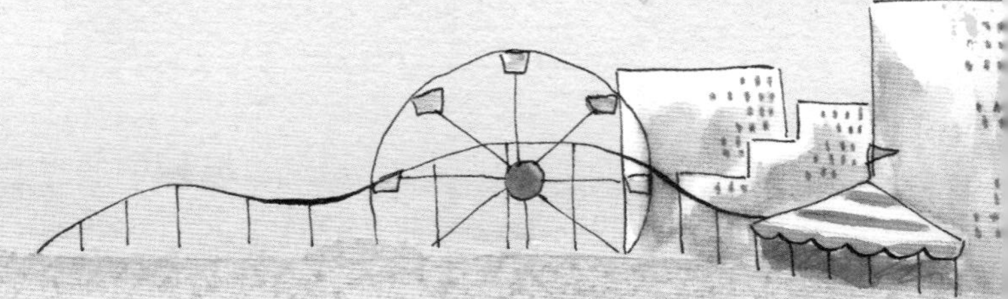

"Come on, Sukie, you can do it!" said Eleanor. She stood at the bottom of the stairs to the beach and waved to Sukie.

But Sukie was just a small dog,

and the stairs were big and sandy,

and she hadn't had lunch yet,

and her foot hurt a little,

and she might get a shell stuck up her nose,

and she might tumble down on her head,

and then she'd need stitches,

and, besides, there might be lobsters.

So Sukie sat at the top of the stairs with
Chunka Munka by her side.

"Oh, all right!" said Eleanor. She picked them both up with a "tsk" and a huff and carried them down the stairs.

“Come on, Sukie, you can do it!” said Eleanor.
She tossed a beach ball Sukie’s way.

But Sukie was just a small dog,

and the beach ball was big and beachy,

and it might hit her nose,

and then it would pop,

and it might be too loud,

or it might knock her down and she might never get up again, and she might have to live on the beach forever and eat seaweed to survive, and, besides, beach balls attract lobsters.

So Sukie sat far away from the beach ball with Chunka Munka by her side.

"Oh, Sukie!" Eleanor swooped that pup up with a "tsk" and a huff and cradled her in her arms.

"Come on, Sukie, you can do it!" Eleanor stood at the water's edge and splashed a little splash at Sukie.

But Sukie was just a small dog,

and those waves were big,

and they were whooshy,

and they were salty, and they were too wet,

and they might toss her out to the middle of the sea,

and she might float all the way to Tasmania
or even Florida,

and she might be swallowed by a whale,

and she wasn't wearing a bathing suit,

and, besides, there might be lobsters.

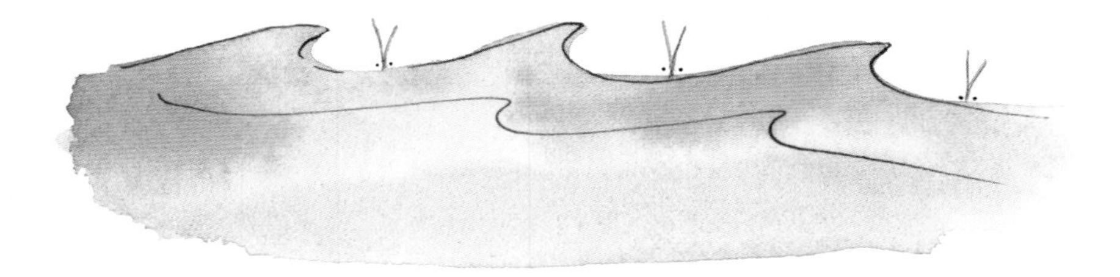

So Sukie sat at the edge of the water with
Chunka Munka by her side.

"Oh, Sukie!" said Eleanor. She shook her head and dove into the waves.

GUARD

Sukie sat and watched beach balls bouncing and big boys running and umbrellas flapping and lifeguards blowing loud whistles and waves splish-splashing with Chunka Munka—

floating out to sea!

Sukie barked for Chunka Munka to come back!

Chunka Munka started to sink.

Sukie started to paddle.

She paddled past a big beachy ball . . .

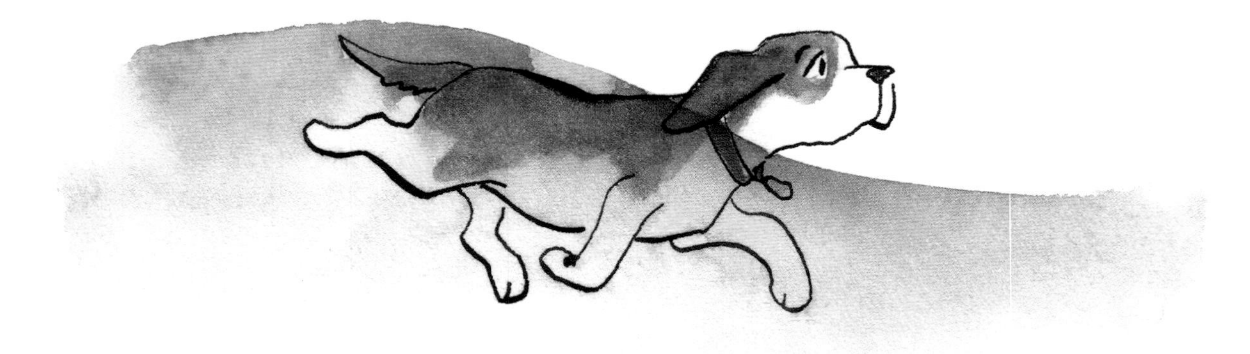

and through a huge salty wave . . .

and over something that might even be a lobster.

Until she had Chunka Munka.
He was safe.

Sukie had saved him.

She felt braver than the bravest dog, because even though she was very small, Chunka Munka was smaller.

"Oh, Sukie, I knew you could do it!" said Eleanor. She picked them both up with a "yay" and a "hooray" and swung them very gently through the air.

Sukie sat in the sandy sand with the wavy waves and watched for lobsters with Chunka Munka by her side.

And they didn’t see one all day.

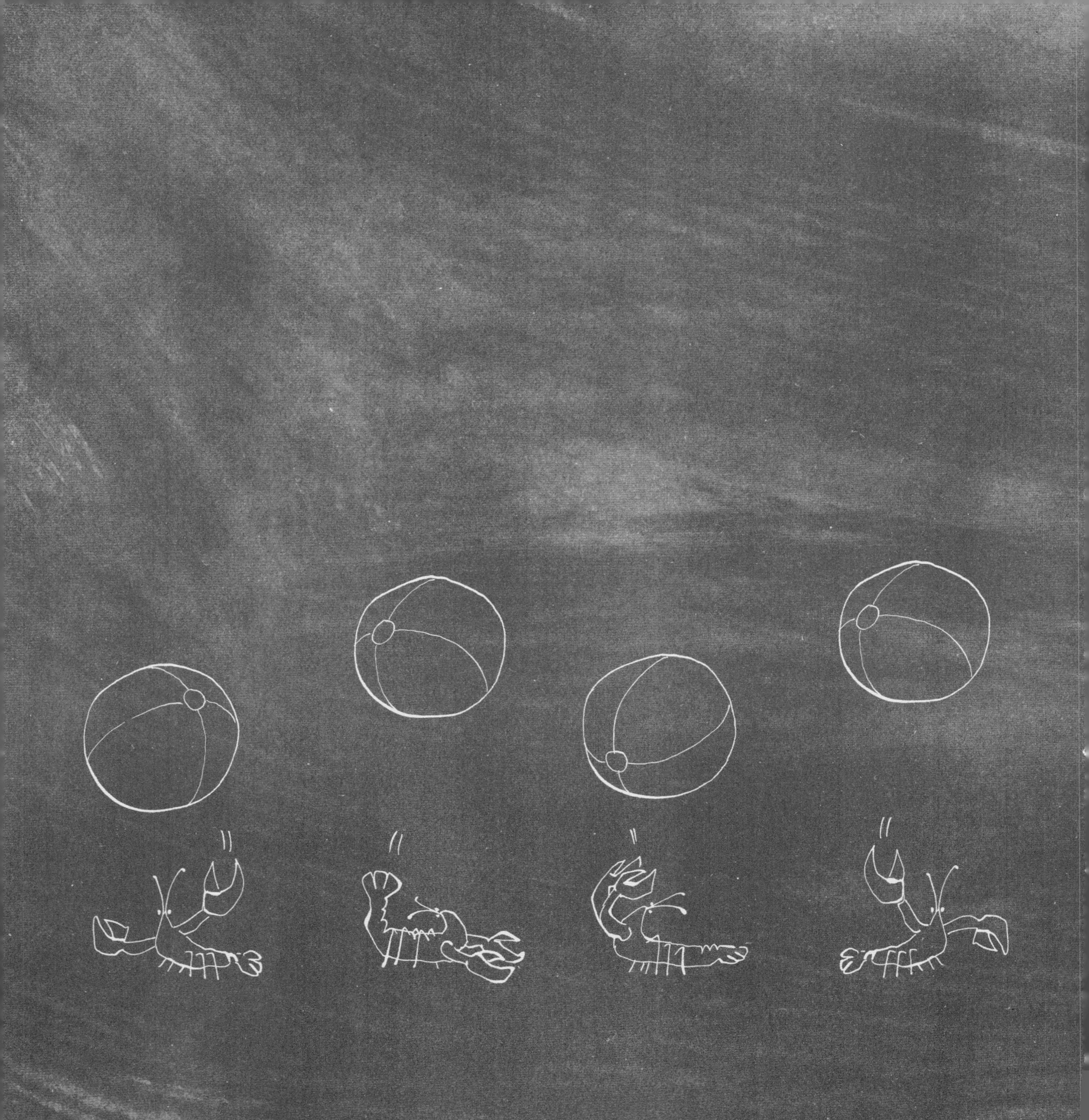